Love,
Joe + Jackie
January, 1993

Love is a great thing, a great good in every wise; it alone maketh light every heavy thing and beareth evenly every uneven thing.

Thomas à Kempis
The Imitation of Christ

IN PRAISE OF LOVE

SMITHMARK

This edition published in 1992 by SMITHMARK
Publishers Inc., 112 Madison Avenue, New York, N.Y. 10016
ISBN 0-8317-5010-3
Printed and bound in Hong Kong
Producer: Solomon M. Skolnick *Designer:* Ann-Louise Lipman
Editor: Joan E. Ratajack *Production:* Valerie Zars
Photo Researcher: Edward Douglas *Assistant Photo Researcher:* Robert V. Hale *Editorial Assistant:*
Carol Raguso

Reprinted by permission of:

Harcourt Brace Jovanovich, Inc.: Antoine de Saint-Exupéry, *Wind, Sand, and Stars,* translated by Lewis Galantière, copyright © 1939. **New Directions Publishing Corporation:** Hilda Doolittle, (H.D.), "Leda," from *Collected Poems, 1912–1944,* copyright © 1982 by the Estate of Hilda Doolittle. Gary Snyder, "Mother Earth: Her Whales," from *Turtle Island,* copyright © 1972 by Gary Snyder. **Paraclete Press:** Thomas à Kempis, *The Imitation of Christ,* edited by Hal M. Helms, copyright © 1982, Paraclete Press, Orleans, MA 02653. **Random House:** Homer, *Odyssey,* translated by Robert Fitzgerald, copyright © 1963. **St. Martin's Press:** Thomas Hardy, *The Hand of Ethelberta,* copyright © 1978. **Suhrkamp Verlag:** Johann Wolfgang Von Goethe, *Iphigenia in Tauris,* from *Goethe: Collected Works,* translated by Robert M. Browning, copyright © 1988.

Index of Photographers

All photographs courtesy of The Image Bank. For information contact
The Image Bank, 111 Fifth Avenue, New York, N.Y. 10003

Shoji Yoshida endpaper. **Steve Dunwell** 4. **Pamela Zilly** 5. **David De Lossy** 7, 11, 12-13, 24-25. **Marcel Isy-Schwart** 9. **Grant V. Faint** 10. **Walter Choroszewski/Stockphotos, Inc.** 14-15. **Elyse Lewin** 17. **Maria Productions** 18 (2). **Zao-Grimberg** 19. **Terje Rakke** 20-21. **Werner Bokelberg/G + J Images** 23. **John Lewis Stage** 26. **William Hamilton** 27. **Maria Taglienti** 28. **Bill Carter** 29.

O Lyric Love, half angel and half bird,
And all a wonder and a wild desire.

Robert Browning
"The Ring and the Book"

Pleasure and love are the pinions of great deeds.

Johann Wolfgang von Goethe
Iphigenia in Tauris

To live is like to love—all reason is against it, and all healthy instinct for it.

Samuel Butler
Life and Love

Love is a driver, bitter and fierce
if you resist and fight him,
Easy-going enough once you
acknowledge his power.

Ovid
The Loves

Love is the only gold.

Alfred, Lord Tennyson
Becket

Ah kingly kiss—
no more regret
nor old deep memories
to mar the bliss

Hilda Doolittle
"Leda"

Come live with me, and be my love;
And we will all the pleasures prove
That valleys, groves, hills, and fields,
Woods or steepy mountain yields.

Christopher Marlowe
"The Passionate Sheperd to His Love"

There is nothing nobler or more admirable than when two people who see eye to eye keep house as man and wife, confounding their enemies and delighting their friends.

Homer
Odyssey

Many waters cannot quench love,
neither can floods drown it.

Song of Solomon 8:7

Age cannot wither her, nor custom stale
Her infinite variety; other women cloy
The appetites they feed; but she makes hungry
Where most she satisfies.

William Shakespeare
Antony and Cleopatra

Love is not to be purchased,
and affection has no price.

Saint Jerome

For Mercy has a human heart,
Pity, a human face,
And Love, the human form divine,
And Peace, the human dress.

William Blake
"The Divine Image"

Love sought is good, but giv'n unsought is better.

William Shakespeare
Twelfth-Night

Thou shalt love thy neighbor as thyself.

Leviticus 19:18

IS man most precious of all things?
—Then let us love him, and his brothers, all those
Fading living beings—

Gary Snyder
"Mother Earth: Her Whales"

Life has taught us that love does not consist in gazing at each other but in looking outward together in the same direction.

Antoine de Saint-Exupéry
Wind, Sand, and Stars

All mankind love a lover.

Ralph Waldo Emerson
"Love"

If ever thou shalt love,
In the sweet pangs of it remember me;
For such as I am all true lovers are:
Unstaid and skittish in all motions else
Save in the constant image of the creature
That is beloved.

William Shakespeare
Romeo and Juliet

A lover without indiscretion is no lover at all.

Thomas Hardy
The Hand of Ethelberta

I shall love you in December
With the love I gave in May!

John Alexander Joyce
"Question and Answer"

All for love, and nothing for reward.

Edmund Spenser
The Faerie Queene

By heaven, I do love,
and it hath taught me to rime,
and to be melancholy.

William Shakespeare
Love's Labour's Lost

Light, love, life

Johann Gottfried von Herder
Epitaph

There is only one happiness in life, to love and be loved.

George Sand
Letter to Lina Calamatta

Whoso loves
Believes the impossible.

Elizabeth Barrett Browning
Aurora Leigh